Steffie and Me

by Phyllis Hoffman
Pictures by Emily Arnold McCully

Harper & Row, Publishers

New York, Evanston, and London

For my mother and father
and brother

My school is big and gray
with wooden doors and a pointy railing
like a castle.
Every day I have to go there.

After breakfast
my friend up the block calls for me.
Stephanie rings four times
so I know who it is.
It's our code.
"She thinks we're deaf!" my brother yells.
I give him a punch
and run to the door.

Stephanie's sister Mary waits outside.
She's afraid to come in
because of our dog.

7

My mother kisses me on the head
and Steffie and I have a race to the bus.
I always win
because Steffie has to stop
and pull up Mary's socks.
I use rubber bands.

8

Our seat is lumpy
with a big hole in the middle.
It's behind the driver.

Once when Stephanie was sick,
I missed our bus
and my brother had to take me.
He held my arm until we met his friends.
Then he made donkey ears on me and walked away.
But when we got to school,
he took me to my door.
I waved to him from my seat.
"Bye, Schrunchkadilly!"
"Bye, Freediemeyer!"
Now everybody knows
I really have a brother.

Our room is on the first floor.
It has lots and lots of windows
with stupid tulips on them.
We made everything that's hanging on the walls.
Except some of the stuff is from last year.

Our teacher is beautiful.
She wears glasses,
and has ruffles on her sleeves.
Her hankie shows.

On assembly day
we have to wear red ties
and line up in size places.
Stephanie is the littlest person in the class
and I'm next, so we're partners.

Our school gave a big talent show
and Steffie and I were in it.
We dressed up like monkeys
and did a tap dance.
In the middle of our song
my costume fell off!
The big kids laughed so hard I could hear them.
But the teachers clapped and clapped
and I got more applause than anybody.
Then my brother stood up
and cheered for me.

TALENT SHOW

My brother is a monitor.
I always see him
going to the lunchroom.
We sneak up behind him
and tickle his ears!
I'm the noisiest one in my whole class
and he never reports me.

My brother wants to be a lawyer
and a garbage collector.

Every day I bring tuna fish and an apple.
When I finish the apple,
I give it to Brucie.
He likes the pits.
Stephanie and I are going to marry him.

17

Once Steffie cried
because her tooth was loose
and she couldn't chew her sandwich.
Miss Burg said she didn't have to
and wrapped it up for later.
We put my coat over our heads
and ate the cookies.

In the afternoon we put aprons on
and Miss Burg gives us finger paint.
It tastes delicious
and it makes your teeth green.

19

I like art because you can tell all your dreams in it.
One day I drew a picture
of my father's moustache!
Then I pasted hair
under my nose
so I looked just like him.
Stephanie said I was handsome.
She's so funny.

20

Before we go home,
everyone has to sing the school song.
We always goof it up.
Oh, One-Fifty-Two
is the very worst school,
deedalee deedalee dum!
I made up the words.

I always go home to see if my mother's there.
She works in the daytime
but sometimes she comes home early.

If she's not around,
I pour a little milk into a glass
and shake it up
so it looks like I had a lot.
Then I go to Stephanie's.

Her mother makes us cocoa.
We drink it from cups with handles.

Stephanie and I play "Chopsticks" on the piano
and write our names on each other's sneakers.
LOULOUBELLE
POOCHIE
Mary can't spell
so I write hers.
FEE FEE

When it gets dark,
I'm afraid to walk home alone.
So my father comes for me.
He gives me a piggyback ride
and I straighten his hat.

25

I hate dinner.
Just because I won't eat the meatloaf,
my mother says I had candy at Stephanie's.

When she gets up to bring seconds,
I push the lumps in my potato
to one side of my plate
and slide them onto my napkin.
My brother never tells because he does it too.

After dinner I play with the junk
in my bottom drawer and do my homework.
Then I put my underwear on the radiator
so it gets hot in the morning.

When it's time for bed,
I put pajamas on my head
and jump around the room,
trying to see myself in the mirror.

I have a scar in the same place as my brother.
We peek at each other through the keyhole.

He goes to bed
the same time as I do.
Otherwise I complain.

My mother tucks me in
even if she's tired.

I always hear noises in the room
so my father comes and turns my light on.
I tell him a story.
"Good night, monkey," he whispers.
Then he sits on the end of my bed
until I fall asleep.